The Postcards I Never Sent is emotive and imaginative, transcending the reader into Patterson's world as she balances intimacy with raw exposure. In this body of work, Patterson honors and navigates the humanity of feminine, fragile, and fertile experiences, in a way that makes the pain and the hope of family and love accessible to us all. She shares her story with a unique delicacy and has created what many of us need: a collective space where the wildest parts of ourselves can both dance and be understood with such clarity. Lyn's writing is a gift and an invitation to explore our personal nuances through the evocative ways she articulates her own.

—Chloe Dulce Louvouezo, author of *Life, I Swear: Intimate Stories from Black Women on Identity, Healing, and Self-Trust*

The Postcards I Never Sent is an explorative and transformative road trip towards healing. Patterson's storytelling is a daring act of vulnerability, exposing the raw, softest parts of personal heartbreak and Black femininity. There is tangible magic metamorphosing in these words as Lyn guides us through her own journey of pain, growth, and fragility; welcoming the reader to embrace the sensuous chaos of being human. Patterson's writing does not shy away from navigating nuanced topics, but rather her voice gracefully undresses them with her needed and important perspective. It is a collection that not only inspires reflection, but the redefining of our relationships with ourselves, others, and home.

—Laura Henebry, 2022 Fable Grant Recipient

Lyn Patterson's writing is a tour de force of movement and rhythm. She so deftly shifts between writing styles all while keeping a cohesive lyrical precision throughout. Through this journey, readers get to witness personal exploration and excavation in many forms. These poems invite the reader to examine the infinite complexities and the subtle nuances of relationships— with our communities, our histories, our loved ones, and ourselves. Patterson has given us a collection that is so sweepingly immersive, I swear I sunk into these pages and then emerged gasping and awestruck on the other side.

—Amy Kay, poet and educator

~~strong~~ black woman.
~~strong~~ black woman.
~~strong~~ black woman.
~~strong~~ black woman.
~~strong~~ black woman.
~~strong~~ black woman.
~~strong~~ black woman.
s o f t black woman.

a line for every ancestor
who had to learn to be
strong before being *soft.*

~ *in dedication*

www.blacklawrence.com

Executive Editor: Diane Goettel
Book Design: Amy Freels
Cover Design: Zoe Norvell
Cover Art: Mickalene Thomas, *Baby I Am Ready Now*, 2007, Diptych, acrylic, rhinestone and enamel on wooden panel, 72 x 132 in. (overall), 72 x 60 in. (left panel), 72 x 72 in. (right panel)

In June of 2023, Black Lawrence Press welcomed numerous existing and forthcoming Nomadic Press titles to our catalogue. The book that you hold in your hands is one of the forthcoming Nomadic Press titles that we acquired.

Published 2024 by Black Lawrence Press.
Printed in the United States.

THE POSTCARDS
I NEVER SENT

LYN PATTERSON

CONTENTS

Dear Reader,

"*Even when it burns /* it's still poetry."

This final couplet from my wife's poem, "The Affair," so remarkably summarizes her approach to poetry and life. Ever since I met Lyn, her soul has been burning. Indeed, it is difficult to imagine her words *not* burning with passion, sincerity, and universal truths, as we follow her through the coming-of-age journey on which she leads readers in *The Postcards I Never Sent*, her second book of poetry.

Page after page, we dance with her through tributes to ancestors; we smile as she cackles in rebellion, in spite of a society that would rather stifle her joy; we mourn with her through loss of love and unattainable lovers; and we behold with reverence and compassion as she experiences the highs and lows of life as a human, woman, black being. Not as the legendary "strong black woman" (though she undeniably is), but, perhaps more profoundly, a black woman whose humanity, dignity, life, and joy do not require justification. Lyn challenges her readers to celebrate and normalize her unapologetic black womanhood. She nods to poetry themes of black struggle and resistance, while asserting herself as a multi-dimensional woman with contemporary priorities.

I gave Lyn a travel journal the day we got married, honestly, quite worried she would never use it. At that point in our shared journey, we were regular travelers, taking annual trips to commemorate anniversaries, in addition to other travel throughout each year. She began writing in that journal about a year later, at a time when we were experiencing relationship difficulties.

Since then, like many other couples, we have had our share of good times and bad, some of which you will read about in this book. We have wondered together if this/we will ultimately work out. We have gone to therapy. We have separated. We have reconsidered monogamy, as well as the institution of marriage. We have bounced back from the brink of catastrophe. Together, we adopted a dog and had a child. We are embracing our imperfections, solo, as well as in tandem.

***

Dear Lyn,

Your soul burns stronger each day as you realize your passions and continue to achieve new heights with your art. Whether you are harmonizing with the ancestors or broadcasting from the epicenter of a side show, you continue to remind us of our connection to things bigger than ourselves. Sometimes we must be burnt down in order to be re-made stronger.

We are still poetry, even when it burns.

Jeremy

12.01.22

INTRODUCTION

As humans, we are inspired by stories of change and metamorphosis. There's no greater symbol of this than the lowly, crawling caterpillar that evolves into the majestic, soaring butterfly. But, to me, the most important part of the story happens during the in-between, quiescent, transformative stage. Oftentimes, when we experience these all-important growth stages, we don't have the right words to move through them. Many of us stay silent, which can cause us to suffer alone. The most compelling storytellers capture these pivotal points when we are broken down to our primordial state and on the cusp of personal revolutions.

Three years ago, I decided to no longer suffer alone, so I stepped out of my cocoon and started a poetry blog on Instagram. As I spewed my rage into the ether, something magical happened. People started to pay attention. They began reaching out to tell me how my words impacted them, how I helped them to process a difficult situation or how my words made them feel less alone. As a result of the community that developed around my work, I was able to publish my first collection of poetry with a small publisher. This experience taught me that there is power in our collective voice and we can create communities of care through shared stories. My favorite poet, Audre Lorde, once said, "Poetry is not a luxury. It is a vital necessity for our existence." Through seeing my words impact others, I learned that poetry has the power to move people's hearts and minds, and thus, it is necessary.

My goal as an author is to tell necessary stories of black existence, unapologetically, with both nuance and simplicity. For far too long, mainstream black storytelling has centered around the narrative of struggle and resistance. But while these aspects of black culture have become salient parts of my identity, woven through my family history, it becomes most interesting when readers are able to see how my identity impacts real human experiences we all relate to. We all want to read books where our heroines fall in love, get their hearts broken, persevere through failure, and stand against evil. We all deserve heroines we can see ourselves in.

In working towards my goal of creating such works of art, I began piecing together the poems of this book, when I began traveling full time. As I bounced from place to place, sleeping on friends' couches, I was able to capture the gradations and peculiarities of everyday life. As I adventured, I observed people intently, tracked my ancestry, collecting family folklore along the way, and witnessed breath-taking landscapes. I wrote these poems either as fragments jotted urgently in my travel journal or as free writes scribbled on napkin scraps.

Even as I read them now, these poems bleed and breathe because I was breaking down and expanding simultaneously. I was a black woman coming of age in America, yearning to be wild and liberated, while attempting to place myself in space and time. I looked for books that would give me solace along my journey. But tales of transformation about a thirty something year old, nearly divorced, self-proclaimed wild woman, who fits in everywhere and nowhere, were hard to find. Black women in particular don't often find these adventurous, coming of age stories set in the American writer's landscape. So, I set out to capture my story in honor of my friends, my aunties, my mother, my grandmother, and for the daughters of the future to remember us by. Because truly great narratives connect people in the past, present, and future.

When I think about stories of transformation and revolution, I am reminded that we are all connected to a greater collective memory, which brings me back to my favorite symbol, the butterfly. After an astonishing metamorphosis, newly-winged Monarch butterflies miraculously begin a migration cycle from the North to the South, one that spans five to six generations of butterflies. No one truly understands how they know to migrate every fall, but the dutiful children of previous generations continue the migration, completing their life cycle before reaching the final destination. They do this because they belong to one another, just as humans do. Please never forget that our stories have the power to guide us as we persevere through our own metamorphoses, while also reminding us of our divine connections to something bigger.

Thanks for reading.

Dear Jeremy

Baltimore, MD

On the day we got married you gave me this beautiful travel journal to remind me of the promise you made in our vows. That you'd always support my need to be free and be by my side even when you could not physically be here. I am finally using the journal, and slightly hoping it finds its way back to you.

AN UNRELIABLE NARRATOR

She is a howling creature
on a mission, crawling to

collect her dreams from
drowning down the
bathroom sink with the
"all natural" deep conditioner.

She's some nocturnal animal
in search of her sisters

finding her luminescence
in the light of the moon.

She's a platform pedaling beauty,
sweating her edges out from
nine to five these days

and getting used to living
for the weekend,

though she still never
checks her phone
before noon.

She's a silk cap, bonnet
type, former club queen.

She swears she's just
"in between" things

for now.

Red is the color of sex.

When little girls
become ready peach &
pear shaped women

when the hymen
breaks and the cherry
drips its juice onto the bed

when forgetful minds
skip a pill and your
"friend" misses a visit

when the placenta
bursts and new life comes
furiously into the world.

Red is the color of life and love.

WORDS LIKE WET

Like the squishy soil of a well-manicured plant.

Like paint drying on the artist's canvas, casing over itself.

Like a street after summer rain, slick with the heavy smell of earth.

Like the juice of mango or watermelon dripping down your throat.

Like the flow of the river Oshun, silent, still, sensual.

Like the fiery tongue of a young love, salivating and unquenchable.

Like the speckled dew drops dripping on fall and winter leaves.

Like a salty bead of sweat seeping from eyes down to tongue and cheek.

Like an ice cube melting slowly on the warmth of a palm.

Like the orange sun meeting the ocean at the breaking of dawn.

Like hot water in a bath or bubbles in the tub.

Like steam on a champagne glass or honey melting in a tea mug.

Sometimes my words are full like molasses—smooth, subtle, and thick.

Sometimes my words are sweet like candy—mouth-watering, sticky, and wet.

MY WAR CRY

I've never cared
much for rules.

I need to know
who makes them.

And what happens
when I break them...

WILD WOMAN
SISTERHOOD

If you're going to
meet me for coffee
you should know

that I'm always
running late

because I rebel
(even against the
institution of time).

If you're going to
confide in me
you should know

I'm learning to be
a little gentler with
the truth even though

I am deeply committed to it.

If you're going to
conversate with me

I hope you can accept
that it *is* in fact a word,

one we say when
code switching.

I hope you
welcome its use.

Being friends with wild women
is therapy to a soul rebel.

When we come together
we do not giggle.

Instead, we cackle like
it's part of our senses,

deep from the soul
up through the belly.

The way wolves
howl up at the moon.

Mom says I didn't always move like wildfire.
"You took a few steps on your first birthday but
you wouldn't walk until you were certain."

Dear Jeremy

Seattle, WA

I think you were right. Our marriage cannot continue like this. When I look back at all the time that's come and gone, I wonder how I have become the person I have become. A person who has done many of the things my parents used to do to each other.

THE BORROWING

There are women who raised
the women who raised you.

This is the borrowing of bones.

There are men that never knew
you never knew them.

This is the borrowing of ribs.

Going through old photos
in a shoebox, with my mom.

There's a picture of me at fifteen
which makes her pause.

She says, "We were smarter
than that back in my day,

we didn't take pictures so
we couldn't get caught."

I respond, "Well, somebody
had to be paying attention
for me to get caught."

We giggle because
it's the truth, even though

it was a lifetime ago.

There is still a
heaviness there.

A pain in the silence
that fills the room.

Even though we swear,
"We're better now…"

MOM AND I ARE
STILL HEALING

RUM AND STARDUST

Maybe addiction is not
a generational curse.

Perhaps we're all just
made of stardust

and uninspired by the earth.

Maybe we're just
looking for a way out

and we need to, at least,

feel

how high we fly
before we reach the dirt.

SHATTERED GLASS

I do not know how to
handle things with care

because I am still raw
from the trauma.

I can shatter shit into
one million pieces.

Easily.

But I am still learning
how to put it all back.

Together.

JACKSON ST

My parents' love language
was too often war,

and I have the scars
to prove it, therefore

I've never "believed"
in the sanctity
of forever, because

I think people should
come and go freely,

as they please.

Besides, sometimes

it's leaving

that is the ultimate
act of love.

STORIES ABOUT LEAVING

I'm used to writing
stories about leaving;

Matching t-shirts with our
faded faces stuffed deep
in a catch-all drawer.

A crumpled dollar bill hidden
behind an old photo with
my initials and an IOU.

The empty bottle of Bacardi
Gold my sister poured down
the drain each day,

sometime after I came home
from school and before
I moved East for good.

I said, I'm used to writing
stories about leaving.

I've packed more suitcases
and storage bins in five years

than friends I've made along the way
whose couches were my bedroom

on restless nights when I was
busy chasing after myself.

I said, I'm used to writing
stories about leaving.

At any point in time if I see a red
flag or something I don't like

just know, I've already got
my bags packed in my mind.

I said, I'm used to writing
stories about leaving.

These last ten years may have
brought some of us sobriety, but

I was forced to say more
goodbyes in my little lifetime

than I've been willing to wait
around for an "I'm sorry."

I said, I'm used to writing
stories about leaving.

I've listened to bag lady
at least 2,000 times so
I know how to pack light

and I haven't found
one city with enough
personality to keep me,

so I buy flowers from the grocery store
every week, not because they're beautiful

but because they remind me that
everything wonderful
is impermanent.

I said, I'm used to writing
stories about leaving.

Therefore,

my air force ones are tattered and
worn because I never learned

how to say, "I forgive you."
Instead, I take off…

and I'd quite like to rewrite this
old history, so this story

is about the time I stayed.

the sun is always whole but even it cannot stop a half-moon from swallowing it whole when the night sky folds.

Dear Jeremy

Greenville, SC

Today was the first time I thought about divorce. Everything is just so tense. My head is spinning with all of the wrongs that have transpired between us. I don't trust you. You don't trust me and I am exhausted from fighting. I am not even sure what we are fighting for anymore.

BRUSHING OUR TEETH

"Nobody dies from
pain," he says.

"True,"
I respond.

Truth is, some
people are better

from the suffering
but some are broken.

Truth is, these are
the same people.

TIME OF DEATH

My lover and I discuss
the time of death

for descendants of
Adam vs Lilith.

"For men
it's old age."

"But, for women
it's marriage."

He still doesn't
get why I don't
believe in it. But,

we have so much
more time for the

wishes to age

into regrets.

OUR BED IS
NEVER MADE

I'm on nights and…
you're on days.

Sins of the past paint
the fitted sheets in stains.

While sticks and stones

echo loud enough to
decorate the hallways.

The kitchen's got a stench,
which is not coming from
the compost bin.

The milk's expired
and my flowers are
never watered.

This palace was once
our oasis, now it is a

concrete manifestation
of our daily chaos.

SHARP OBJECTS

I.

My father used to
train me in the dark.

He'd turn off all the lights
and simulate an attack
from different angles.

Then he'd flip on the switch,
grab my shoulders and demand

I name the nearest items that could be
used to defend myself against him.

I guess I'm still cautious and
always looking for the
sharpest object.

II.

When I found out
what you had done,

I broke every piece of
china we ever owned,

& for weeks, we
couldn't walk around

the house without
the shards of glass

pricking us both in the feet.

It was a piercing reminder that you
had transformed yourself into

the sharpest of all the
objects I've encountered.

III.

Every man
I've ever loved
has been just
a little bit rough—

well-intentioned maybe
but still a weapon

*of my own self
destruction.*

I was bad but you were worse
and better at it, I might add.

Yes, there were affairs and
the betrayal was deep.

I wore my bridal lingerie for him
and you let her wear the sweater
I bought you on our honeymoon.

That's just what happens

sometimes

when you get married,

you get caught in this never
ending cycle of scrubbing

DIRTY LAUNDRY

THE AFFAIR

You broke my heart
and it's heavy

because I still
love you enough to

make beautiful things
even out of your flaws

even when they hurt me.

For you, I always
find the words

even when it burns
it's still poetry.

HOWE ST

Howe St. must be
a penitentiary

for virtuous kings who
have lost all their glory.

Howe St. must be
a tunnel of darkness,

an infirmary for sorry
ass men and an echo
chamber of melancholy.

Howe St. must be
a cemetery

where dying men come
to rest their weary heads

before Lilith rips them from
their rib, and tears
them to shreds.

Howe St. must be
a hollow place

filled with sadness
and sin.

SPACE

Space—like limitless
intergalactic darkness.
The unknown realm
of possibility which excites
and terrifies the mind.
An organism which cannot
fathom its own infiniteness.

Space—like the kind
you took up at my place.
A toothbrush next to the sink,
the briefs in my laundry, and
on the nightstand the novel
you were currently reading.
All of which brought
me light beams, when
the moon was honey.

Space—like the kind that
fills the void of silence.
Hanging like an eerie fog.
Ready to swallow us
into oblivion, though I'm
not ready to step into the
void just yet.

THE PURGE

shells for ancestors/ because my
grandmother always taught me how
profound it was to put your ear to the
ocean/ how to find joy in realizing
how small we truly are/

stones for presence/ because
becoming unburdened is heavy/ and
it requires the weight of our stillness/

glass for breaking/ because once
something is broken it can never be
put back together but the mourning
of what was lost will remain rage
ready to gut you from the inside out
if you don't release it

friends to scream at the ocean
alongside you/ because even though
you are a fortress built from glass
and stones/ you can still be knocked
down by the crashing wave of
darkness/ if you try to suffer through
this alone

blessings and offerings for the
season/ may this fresh start be the
brightest of summer mornings/

it can be so hard to see beauty
when things are broken/

but without destruction there is no
room for rebuilding here.

Flippant words speak louder than actions.
Shallow words. Words that hollow.

Dear Jeremy

Philadelphia, PA

I am beginning to unravel. These last few weeks have been heavy. Diving into the deep has forced me to deal with so many memories around abuse and trauma that I have suppressed for decades. Some have been buried so deep that I had forgotten they were there.

MALAISE

What does it matter if it rains
What does it matter if it rains
What does it matter if it rains
What does it matter if it rains
What does it matter if it rains
while   you   are   drowning?

SHADOW WORK

This is the season
of forgotten
personification

for the thought
provoking flower.

They are wilting
and it's not beautiful
or graceful

but it is a part
of their power.

DEAR STARS,

High above

lend me
your wrath.

The way you
shine in darkness

and fly, even
when you fall.

If the truth can break it,
then let it crumble.

If the truth can start a fire,
then let it burn.

If the truth makes it rain,
then let it pour.

If the truth gives you freedom,
then start a fucking war.

HANDPRINTS

Handprints. Tend. Ache. Grasp. Yet. No one really knows. Which came first. Or which will be the last. All we are certain of is that we are trapped. In a very mundane episode of the twilight zone. Where the weeks drag like a dead man's footprints in the sand. And no one goes insane. It's crazy. We recognize that language is so telling of the mind. Especially within the last few hours of sunrise. But there are lots of tired women on death row scared that even the slightest breeze could carry their imprints far from home. For we are but a blip in time. Indebted to the rule of thumb. Even our idioms are a shrine. To the collective trauma we are all working to overcome.

Handprints. Grip. Clench. Bruise. Our calloused knuckles and sweaty palms. Symbols of ignorance. The eulogy for all of humanity. Our thumbs become the master's tools. Eyes for the blind. A voice for the deaf. And mute. While our poem titles become clickbait. Our mouths, traitors. And our fingertips. weapons of mass destruction. The highest achievement of human evolution. Just clacking away. Equating over indulgence with abundance. Having more instead of being it. A list of indifference on the lightness of being. Even the "hand that wrote it all" eventually fades to a speck of dust. In the great big swirl.

Handprints. Redden. Palpate. Hold. We learn to reap what we sow. So we ask the sun to make us wind. Fight for the mirage of optimism. And hope becomes a tricky thing. For it can transmute itself into anything. Even a corpse or carcass, when left to lurk. Linger. Or rot. It can permeate all our false starts. And dot, dot, dot. The only thing we truly own is the present. We must learn to honor it. Aware that even the earth could one day be a moon. Because even the daylight changes its mind. But our inability to let go will lead to our stagnation. If we allow it. Ignore the fist when it's ready to loosen its grip. And the clench of our fingertips will be a barometer of the scars and bruises left behind. By our handprints.

*I am an amalgamation of working-class
people forced from their homelands to turn
the soil of a new earth with calloused hands.*

Dear Jeremy

Austin, TX

I am worn. I think I am beginning to realize that I work too much. Struggle with perfectionism. Try to fix everyone's problems and end up neglecting myself in the process. I am worn and tired. But life keeps moving. Despite everything. Life keeps moving.

Daddy said,
"Treat people
the way you want
to be treated."

Mama said,
"Love somebody
more than they can
love themselves."

Nobody taught me
that I am a person
who can be a
somebody to
myself.

LESSONS IN
SELF-CARE

they say people learn
the best lessons from

their failures but

black women have never
been allowed to be

anything but excellent
when a seat at the
table is presented

my therapist & I
both ponder

"is there trauma lurking
in black girl magic?"

HYMNALS

Black women
are nightingales—

unsung heroes in the
trenches of a war

for both gender
and racial equity.

Yet we still shine.

Trust us when
we say,

we know why

caged birds still sing
magnificent songs.

AM I TOO, AMERICA?

I am…Transatlantic cargo American. I am…Irish-Catholic famine American. I am seeking reparations, caravan along the Mississippi, "we will sponsor you," first and second great migration American. I am wade in the water, emancipation proclamation, "I have a dream", crack epidemic, hip hop raised me, zero tolerance, black lives matter, and say her name American. I am South Carolina (probably), but most definitely Hendersonville, North Carolina American. I am Altheimer, Arkansas American. I am Iowa, Montana, Chicago, Philadelphia, Seattle, Sacramento, Baltimore, New York City, Oakland, Californian American. I am military brat, oh beautiful for spacious skies, and from every mountainside American. I am slave, negro, colored, Afram, black (and proud) American. Also, Gaelic, Irish, Irish Catholic, white, Mulatto, mixed, bi-racial, multi-racial, multi ethnic American. I am Shepard, rancher, cowboy, caretaker, secretary, cotton picker, sharecropper, taxi driver, mid-level manager, caregiver, air force veteran, unemployed, professor becoming a doctor American. I am the American Dream, pull yourself up by your bootstraps, and also gentrification is violence American. I am immigrant. I am immigrant, much love to my First Nations people, but not one native bone in my body immigrant. By force and by famine, I am immigrant American. Somewhere between, "I too, am America" and…am I too, America?

PATRIOT

Hardened ebony hands
pick apart strands
of a blood-stained flag.

Some days, eager.
Some days, worn.

But never idle

nor destroying
the entire cloth.

*"ain't no such thing as a white
savior, even Jesus wasn't white."*
—*african american proverb*

Dear Jeremy

Minneapolis, MN

A lot of things are birthed through pain. Finding myself in space and time has led me to believe that I carry so much of my ancestors' pain and glory. Patterns which repeat themselves in nations, communities, and families. The entire world feels like it is coming undone alongside me, and still all I can think about is you.

SIDEWALK CHALK

All summer long
little ones write

messages of optimism
in chalk to decorate
the sidewalks

but

no one in Jingletown
writes about
black bodies

and

the concrete
is so very silent
for black lives

unless

our silhouettes
paint the pavement
with white outlines.

THE CLOTILDA SONNET

Black is hard to get out of bed in the morning.
Black as worn down as tired ballet flats.

Gods and mothers. Fighting for their share
of the american dream after midnight.

Language is a fabric that binds us. The souls of
Black folk, we've learned to cloak in english.

African beyond measure. Baptized somewhere deep below
the mason dixon, a place I've never called my home.

Occult rituals. African-american mysticism. Heritage
stewardship. Oral legacies rooted in our survival.

So what. If maybe. I am a fucking bastard with
no knowledge of my father's tribal tongue.

Black is easy to slip into after a hard day's
work pulling at your boot straps.

Black as effortless as cotton and coconut oil.

AMERIKKKA IS AN ASHY BITCH & I'M FINNA READ HER FOR FILTH

Amerikkka, I want a revolution, but I'm so
tired of fighting you, until my skin scars and
the bruises turn red...white...and blue.

You always say shit like "not right now" &
then criticize me. You meet peace with
violence, even when we kneel peacefully.

But you'll make martyrs out of gun toting
terrorists while calling children thugs and
criminals because their skin has melanin.

Amerikkka you really out here showing yo ass

& just so you know, you can't call it a
fucking coup when the police take selfies
with the militia & are the ones who remove
the barricades so the traitors can get through.

Have you ever read a history book outside of
what they teach you in school? Good lord,
Amerikkka you got us all out here looking
like imbeciles.

& I'll admit, I've been afraid to even write
this, because Amerikkka would rather turn
her body camera off so she can put a bullet in my
back for saying too much.

I wish we could ask Henry Dumas what they
do to poets who use their words to shine a
light on the sins of killer cops...

But I'm tired and I've had e-fucking-nough,
So I'm going to read your bitch ass for every
last one of my ancestors, who had to
swallow their tongue, just to ensure they
could make it home.

We just want to take a knee or go to sleep at
night knowing that our lives are worth more
than a wall sprayed by stray bullets, you
coward ass bitch.

THIS IS A·mer·i·kkk·a,

where the white imagination of "legal" gun
owners and "nice" white ladies walking on
their lunch break are actually the weapons
of mass black destruction we stream
every night on our iPhone screen.

This is a punk ass country, where we have
been fighting for our bodies more than 100
years after securing our freedom (in
writing).

Yet, all we see on TV is black death and
Black culture being consumed in
mass quantity.

Tell me, how can I, too, sing America when I
am a refuge with no home to return to
& I can never fucking forgive or forget that
you did that to me & my ancestors.

Tell me, how can I envision a future here for
my own children without trauma,

when even these white liberals at my job
who claim they support the cause seem to be
annoyed more with the number of emails
our CFO sends or doesn't send with regards
to "current events" than they seem to be
concerned about breaking bread with white
supremacists over Thanksgiving dinner...

(with no fucking mask during a global
pandemic).

In the Amerikkkan tradition, "we don't talk
politics" because "things get heated." But,

what a privilege it is to be so god·damn
ambivalent

when another human being's cold dead body
is outlined in chalk by their murderers on the
mo·ther·fu·cking concrete.

But you're color blind though... so you stay
silent. Even though everybody else can see,
it has always been black and white with you.

Amerikkka, you are the mo·ther·fu·cking gas
lighting queen.

Home of the brave, land of the free and
enslaved.

The hypocrisy. The normality.
The audacity of it all.

At this point, I am just so disgusted
with you to tell you the truth.

A big fuck you to A·mer·i·kkk·a,
I am tired of wasting breath on you.

A small state, too tight
to fit a traveler's pin

surrounded on all sides
by enemies sworn to
destroy them.

In the north, a seaport
inaccessible to a little girl
without a passport.

Living in limbo, a sort
of un-citizenship.

Two states with no resolutions.

A conflict where no one wins.
Two roses and no meat.

AN AIR OF DIPLOMACY

THE FIRST EPISTLES OF ADAM

The Wealth of a Nation begins with
the condemned children of Eden.

Remember, "Abel bore
no sons or daughters."

Therefore,

the principal theory which
governs this existence

(of good and evil)

has become instead a question
(of scarcity and excess).

Another Adam gave birth to this
generation of consumers, but

he wed both Eve and Lilith before
he indulged in the fruit from
the Tree of Knowledge.

BUSINESS CLASS

I reflect deeply
in public places,
pondering how to
disrupt spaces
filled with
belligerent men
who hog
simple things
like armrests,

extending themselves
and hoarding cavities
which belong to me,

however unintentional
they may seem...

Some of our white picket fences are corroding with once distant memories. A dream; the pursuit of happiness, life, liberty, and a promise to be free. Sometimes these white fences feel more like cages, enslaving us to a fantasy.

Dear Jeremy

Miami, FL

Whenever I think of the future without you, it sounds like a dystopian sort of life in my head. This is our adventure. Please allow yourself to be part of it. Allow this time away from home to be the separation we need from our past in order to rebuild a new future.

CHASING SUMMER

I got two Arizona iced teas
from our store on the corner.
I used your phone number
to save my two cents.

Went back to our empty apartment,
put on the show you made me promise
never to finish without you and

I wondered if you felt discontent
with the way it ended.

I stared at your contact in my phone
for as long as it took me to read
your name what felt like 22 times.

For better judgment
I managed to sleep
on a stale bed sheet
in the thick of summer heat,

huddled on my side out of habit
though I felt your weight
especially in your absence.

depression naps and mumble raps/
dick appointments and waiting to
exhale moments/

a new hobby and a revenge body/
uber eats miracles and insomnia
chronicles/

womb healing workshops with
moon manifestations/ breathing
exercises and meditation messages/

dark lane demo tapes (cause the
demons been hella moody)/
rhinestone restraints and fenty
lingerie/

tinder stories and peach emojis/
whisky dick with a side of weed
and honey/

love hangovers from younger
admirers/ moonlit silhouettes
and chatty lyft drivers/

global pandemics and national
epidemics/ feet to the hardwood at
the rising of the sun and a deep sigh
before I finally shut my eyes/

post break up playlist

"i can't breathe" from all the smog
in the sky/ but all you can do is
simply stay black and try not to die

DOING DONUTS

Labyrinths of joy on asphalt; like the
gleeful chalky lines of hopscotch,
which decorate our summer sidewalks.

Round rotundas of vigorous jovial
resistance. Symbols of our fresh-faced
resilience.

Some things just don't need to be
explained;

like why mama's macaroni always
smacks,

or the jittery goodness of young love's
first taste of brown sugar and molasses,

eating the pavement is spiritual and
there's a reason why we call it soul
food.

The screech of skid marks and the
stench of burning rubber seeps into our
senses. Reminding us that life is more
than just a hamster wheel.

That we are more than specks of dust
trapped in the pull of the great big
swirl. And it is our God given right to
be this young and reckless.

So, we bend the concrete, rotate the rear, peel back, and pray that we don't wipe out.

Because even though there is so much waiting for us ahead, there is even more uncertainty about what's coming next.

That's why we always pour out a little bit of henny before we fight our never-ending battle with gravity.

For we are growing aware of the fact that we are stuck in a cycle of endings and beginnings that not everybody wins. And before we meet our end, we flirt with our own immortality.

You see, it is an evolutionary need of man to posture. Thus, we spell out our names in an infinity of endless arrays, that reminds everyone who passes this way, that we were here.

With each spin we are teetering on the cusp of whiplash, destiny, or destruction. Writing the eloquent language of our rage in the dirt.

For it could be so easy for us to be thrown from this orbit. But for this moment,

we are the epitome of time itself.
Rotating around the sun and leaving
our mark emblazoned in the Earth.

WARM BODIES

I am Zoe Kravitz
in High Fidelity

Drunkenly searching for comfort
(in all the wrong places) because
it's easier to be self-destructive
and slay zombies

rather than owning the karma
& dealing with all your trauma
(like a fucking adult)

32, Aries moon,
interested in

one night of mischief
in various forms,

a bit of a mess but
I promise it'll be fun

while it lasts…

Currently looking for
warm bodies.

Rage is easier than grief
Rage is easier than grief
Rage is easier than grief
Rage is easier than grief

Dear Jeremy

New York, NY

I think I am a restless spirit prone to reckless behavior. I am constantly trying to reconcile what it means to be a "wife" while still feeling pulled toward mischief and adventure. I have had to reimagine myself without you and it's finally getting to the point where it doesn't feel *all* bad.

HONEY
DRIPPING

Some drip,
some stick,

others devour
it until there's

nothing left to lick.

Give it to them
until they plead.

Make them beg
until it stings.

Sometimes

I don't know if
I'm the honey

or the bee.

RHINESTONE
RESTRAINTS

Don't get me wrong
I'm into the freaky shit.

I'm talking whips, cuffs, chains,
and rhinestone restraints.

I'll let you
        tie
            me
                up.

But give me lust
and give me glitter.

Give me glitz and
give me glamour.

You make me shiver…

I'll make it shimmer.

TO THE MAN ON THE TRAIN

You are my type. You got that nice, clean, fitted cap, reppin where you're from; Some concrete jungle that's made you wild and strong. Ready to seize your dreams by any means.

That's right, you. You are my type all the way down to those shoes with the swoosh, jump man logo on the tongue. Headphones dialed in to the mindset you're manifesting this season. Likely, a fresh outlook to match an auspicious tapered fade. Those Zircon square studs (for good luck), and that (humble) thin gold chain.

You barely smile but when you do the essence of tea tree oil and "shea butter, baby" fills the room. Every morning I'm glued, (ready to bat my eyelashes at you). But you don't have time for distractions (clearly). Though you may be in need of a peaceful sanctuary... A sturdy place for you to rest, both your head and all those sweet dreams, you've been too busy chasing to even notice me or look my way.

I can just envision you at the end of a long day. Sitting next to me on the sofa, drinking chamomile tea, sometimes spiked with honey (and on weekends with Crown Royal or a few too many shots of Henny). My pearly white toes draped across your legs and before we fall to the stars, we'd make love in our silk scarves and durags. To the man on the train, you are my type.

Evening silhouettes intertwined in passionate sex. Shadows at dawn awaken to sun beams. We had a good run and the rest was great.

Let's not let the hangover dreams tempt fate. I'll take my coffee straight, no milk, no sugar, no agave substitute. I'll take my high heeled shoes, (my scarlet letter news), (to heavy-eyed uber drivers who recognize my midnight blues).

Oh daylight, don't seep in so soon. My morning lit silhouette is not quite ready to embrace the luminescent rays and welcome the moonlight into oblivion, just yet...

CASUAL SEX

You treat me like Eve
some blameful sinful
thing you tuck away
for 1am.

I long to be Mary
some unconditional
thing you come home
to lay your head to.

At the end of the day
we meet, when most
lovers are asleep,

both longing for things
we will *never find*
in one another.

nobody loves
a browning stem,

they pause for the buds
and fawn over the
blossoms

thing is I don't much
feel like blooming this
season

flower boy,

will you still love
me when I'm wilting?

FLOWERBOY

This man is a god. In his gray
sweatpants with his Nike slides on.
And, when he meets me by the light of
the moon, he makes my rapture his
diligent ritual. Mind, body, and soul.

Divinely, baptizes my flesh in the
warmth of his palms. While I scream
his supplications and praise his
fingertips with my moans.

He performs this task with such
devotion and reverence…I can't help
but to worship him with my
submission. Give myself wholly as a
precious sacrifice to our sin and our
unction.

And, what a blissful offering it is to
beg such a benevolent being for his
nectar and his skin. As his virtue is
infinitely giving in its indulgence and
in all these sweet moments of
transcendent release…

However fleeting, and reckless.

Sometimes it feels like I am always mourning
something and I have grown tired of running.
Endlessly searching for a home in other people,
places, and things.

Dear Jeremy

Denver, CO

A lot has happened since we gave ourselves permission to meet other people. I am finding my behavior reflected back to me and I don't like it. It is illuminating, clearly, all the ways that I am unhealed and still healing. My therapist says to be softer with myself. I'm leaning into that these days.

RED EARTH

We met between the curtains of
nightfall. Before the glow of dawn.
Before the gloom of the week consumed
us. And we turned the moon to stone.
Red language. Red earth.

You laid your head down in the garden
of Eden. Your hands felt too good when
they touched me. And your lips a little
too soft of a place.

Circe offered her cup to Odysseus.
Oshun gave Shango a taste of her honey.
Eve told Adam to taste the apple. But
nobody blamed *them* when they all
obliged.

I gave you my lap,

but I want you to know what you want
and to decide on your own intentions
because I am tired of being a false idol…
and I am no longer willing to swim in the
ocean where there is no land in sight.

The truth is that sometimes...

you treat my heart like a bull in a china shop.
you treat my heart like a bull in a china shop.
you treat my heart like a bull in a china shop.
you treat my heart like a bull in a china shop.
you treat my heart like a bull in a china shop.
you treat my heart like a bull in a china shop.
you treat my heart like a bull in a china shop.
you treat my heart like a bull in a china shop.

THE BEAST

I am always struck by the way
you seem to pick all the thorn
covered roses from your garden.

Turn them into falling stars in
your palms. Wish upon their
wilted petals and turn the moon
to stone.

I have stopped seeking
answers in constellations, and
resolved myself to the ambiguity
of this labyrinth.

But the truth is, that
sometimes you treat my heart
like a bull stomping around in a
china shop.

And I have lived enough
lifetimes to know that even hope
can be a cruel predilection when

your dreams find their way into
the bruised and bloody hands of
a false idol.

It wasn't the easiest thing to do
because you felt so good. But it was
the thing I did after I saw my pattern
repeating itself.

You came in strong, but not like most
men, who tell me I am a goddess. You
worship me because my mind is
fertile and my lap is soft. And you
need a warm place to rest and find
peace in your burdens.

But one day you will realize that I
won't heal the broken things inside of
you. And usually, I'm the one left
with the weight of this.

But this time, I have learned all of my
lessons. And I have decided to break
free from the pattern.

CALL ME THEN

Call me… Call me when you're certain or
when you've learned to accept that even
the moon pulls at the ocean without asking
it for justification. Call me… Call me
when you've won the never-ending war
between your heart and your head and
when everything in life "makes perfect
sense." Call me when… you've figured
out why I want you to call me Brittney
instead of Lyn. When you're ready to be
something less than lovers but more than
friends. When… you've journeyed to the
edge of the earth in order to hold all of the
answers to life's greatest mysteries in the
palms of your hands; or when you've
finally accepted that the most beautiful
things in this existence are almost always
beyond our comprehension. You… call
me, then.

the slow death of innocence

is the unpleasant overwhelming
stench of decay which permeates the
unwashed dishes in the kitchen sink.
it's the plants, folding in on
themselves. their edges brown and
wilting. it's me, in a pile of silence
staring up at the ceiling. watching the
fan as it turns for what feels like an
eternity. it's me, scrolling through my
iphone photos from july to february
with brand new eyes. as i try to spot
the precise moment when you went
from saint to serpent. the moment
when you began your descent from
the garden of eden. and wondering
how i was too blind to notice. the slow
death of innocence hit me suddenly.
the impact like a brain injury that
changes your ability to process. every
time i go outside it still feels like even
the sun is screaming profanities. and
food stopped tasting like anything. so
i shed. fat. hair. tears. though it's been
two years, i'm still struggling...

to get out of bed. to water the plants.

I started writing you this poem in
the perennial aisle at Home Depot

You see, you pick plants by following
your senses, and on this day, I was
spinning "Kind of Blue" on repeat.

I picked up some aloe for hydration
(from a thirst I can't quite seem to
quench since you left). When I
replanted it, I dug my fingers into the
core of the earth. Memories of the
sweetest things I've ever known came
flooding back to the surface.

I put the fern in the vase we bought just
in case. I guess, I really just needed
something   consistent   and
uncumbersome ... something low
maintenance.

I wish you knew, that there are still
orange carnations on my altar for you

and when they die, I will have mourned
you twice.

THE DANDELION RITUAL

for letting go of dreams
you are no longer manifesting

Need:

Blooming dandelions (the yellow ones) one per each dream you are releasing.

Full grown dandelions (the white ones) one per each new dream you plan to manifest.

Ritual:

Pick the yellow dandelions first. Acknowledge each thing you are letting go of, by saying it out loud. This signifies its importance and the necessity of mourning. Pick full grown dandelions from their root. As you determine each new dream, blow all the seeds, until there are none left. This symbolizes trust in the universe and willingness to allow its flow. Place all dandelions in a vase together on your altar, do not water, let nature take its course. This is a reminder of the cyclical nature of all things.

Home is a place filled with people who knew me, before I knew myself.

Dear Jeremy

Oranjestad, Aruba

I am in a happy little place these days. I've been reminiscing about the first few holidays we spent together. Your auntie's curried chicken, my mother's greens, and all the traditions we were so excited to share with one another. They say when two people get married it's really the coming together of two families.

Little boat, what is it you seek? Is it the evening sun or the glittering sea? Perhaps, it's where they meet? Are you on some adventure to see? Sincerely, gazing from the beach.

THE CARIBBEAN SYMPHONY

Tropical flora sway softly from wind which picks up speed from storm breeze sent from the mountains. Leaves manifest, pristine patterns as humidity cultivates for eyes and ears these soft sweet melodies.

Hummingbird sanctuaries buzz with lively hums and spirited chirps giving soprano bravado with their flighty beaks. Red wings and black mandible create a colorful dance for all to see. Little birds dart to and fro in the tropical heat.

Waves ripple gentle reggae rhythms. No worries, no cares, feet knee deep in the ocean's chorus. Little crabs with square bodies threaten to tickle your feet. As jade seaweed wraps toes, you release a sigh in harmony.

Nighttime crickets whistle and beep. Hidden behind the green of palm tree leaves. Fauna blending into the background of fresh tendrils become one nocturnal sound. Which soothes the restless soul as eyelids become the last curtain call.

AUNTIE GINA'S HOUSE

This chicken is made with
Soca and hot peppers.

The callaloo mixed
with crab and calypso.

Under the Obatala
a plate of rice and peas
(or peas and rice)

depending on
the mouth eating.

The base of
the table juice
is passion fruit

with essence of
vanilla extract.

In the kitchen,
you won't find no
recipe book.

Just an old stereo and
the freshest ingredients
from her garden.

No salt, no pepper
needed.

ON A HOT SUNNY
DAY IN RENTON

I lament and rejoice
for every time you

bask in joy

it is an act
of activism—

a small battle in a
centuries long
revolution.

For, black boy joy
is its own kind

of magic.

FAMILY HEIRLOOMS

My nephews feed me
chicken and peas from
their Mattel kitchen.

They're four and two but
they already know how
to season their food.

Before they could walk,
they danced in their
mama's belly

Baduizm blasting
on papa's speakers.

In gramma's kitchen
the smell of sweet starch.

Though they may be boys now
one day they'll be men,

"two cornbread lovin brothas"

They are learning to communicate
their preferences by pointing at the
sweet potato pie or the pound cake.

Macaroni & greens they do not eat
just yet but soon they will…

& they'll never forget
the way chitlins smell,

as we bless them
in preparation

for another new year.

I'm starting to dance like someone's favorite tia. (The one who moved too cool and smooth to give you a smile, unless you truly earned it.) I take smaller steps these days so I never have to overcompensate for someone who's got fancy turns, but trips over the rhythm. If I sense danger, I won't give them my arms. Far too many close calls has taught me to be wary if there are too many dips and tricks. I endure… The half smiles and eyes that linger for a moment too long seeking an adventure, (I'm not sure I have in me anymore.) But I never regret it. For the one time each night, I meet a dancer that's not married to the slotted frame. Those with claves in their blood. There's just something about *sabor* that must be birthed in you.

MY COUSIN SAID SHE
SAW YOU ON BUMBLE

and I must admit
it made me smile.

She sent me a screen
shot of your profile and

you just look so…
happy;

like you've been
working out, and
eating healthy…

I must admit it hurt me,

when you blocked
me on everything.

Though I understood,
after I had done, what
I did to you.

But I swear, you didn't
have to be such a
Gemini about it.

You must agree, you share
some of the blame in

causing me to leave…

because you could never
be honest with me about
how you felt.

Now here you are, searching
for love on the internet

while I am here with
someone else &

I'm disillusioned because
this is not the way
we thought things
would turn out to be

when we were young

but both of us just look
so damn happy, in all

our profile pictures.

I don't say I'm resilient anymore (on job interviews) because I'm not sure . . . If it was due to nature or lack of nurture . . . I'm not sure if I have always been a cactus . . . or if I am in fact a rose which had to learn to grow thorns. I'm just not sure . . .

Dear Jeremy

New Orleans, LA

It was so nice to receive your letter. Being apart in disrepair is difficult but I felt encouraged after reading your reflections. I have always known that you are a place that I want to rest my head. But I guess, one of my biggest lessons from our time apart, is that I am finally learning to be a safe space to myself.

LA LA LAND

It's Sunday, Saxophone Colossus
spins on our record player.

We make love as the sun comes up
and cuddle under the warmth of
its beams.

In the living room the fragrance of
roses calls. So, we peel ourselves
out of bed around 10 AM.

I make you waffles for breakfast as
you rub on my booty.

We go for a walk near the water
and giggle when we see the
neighbors (wondering if they
heard us earlier that morning).

We disagree; on which anime to
watch or where to eat but like
always we enjoy the banter.

Before we go to sleep, you kiss me
on the forehead and call me your
angel.

*All you want to do is love on me, all
I want to do is write you poetry.*

if i could plant you

in my garden...i
would make sure
you could always
face the sun.

i would water
your roots with
my tears. and turn
the soil beneath you
with my palm.

i would place you
under the brightest of
stars, for times if our
ephemerality should ever
give you pause.

And in times when the
sky is gray and foggy
or if you fear i might
have moved on.

Know, the thing about
planting flowers in your
garden is that they only
bloom for a season.

So...
you could never
truly be lost.

But above all things
uncertain and muddled
i hope you never forget
just this one…

That if i could plant
you in my garden…
i would. Simply.

and i am learning that
this is enough.

NOSTALGIA

The sky is starless tonight
in the big of the city.

The smog is ever overwhelming.

Your feet are planted
firmly in front of me.

But we both know that
you are daydreaming

of a sunset probably
somewhere near
Los Angeles…

I can smell the
Pacific Ocean on
you now even as

I drift into a fantasy.

I am always thinking of you.
Running freely in jungles
filled with concrete.

Some nocturnal creature,
searching for something wild
beneath the galaxy.

And I know that one day
you will find yourself
under this same sky

finally thinking of me,

and I hope your dreams
are bittersweet

and the memories
just as flawed.

// SMOG

Smog is not the sum total of my being. But it has become synonymous with my name and my undoing. At the women's center on campus we say, "we all breathe in the same smog." At the black student union after class we say, "we all breathe in the same smog." I wonder who among them feels the weight on my lungs (these interlocking systems of oppression), the sum total of my smog.

Smog is my contemplation at the blond hair and blue eyes in *Seventeen Magazine* at twelve. Smog is my lurch at the chemicals in the salon. Smog is my shout at men who put their hands on the small of my back when they pass by me in the blurry strobe lights of the club. Smog is my blood on the white bed sheet at fifteen.

Smog are my tender love letters to boys in juvenile detention centers called "Black Boy Joy."

Smog are the tears of my mascara on the pillowcases to match the sheet.

I wonder if smog was my cry, in the operating room, when the doctor spanked the baby to make sure it could survive in this new world. Worse, was smog my first home, maybe not the sum total of my being but the air my mother breathed into that desolate womb.

The smog I breathe is a heavy fog over the Bay bridge in the winter.

///

Sistas remind one another that we are the dirt of the world. Not smog (never smog) but coffee colored soot. Limbs and arms which form a forest full of greenery and trees. They remind me that, despite the fact that the air can be so violent, I still have so much that needs saying. That you will find it hard to speak when you can't breathe, but there is much more pain in silence.

They remind me that smog isn't actually words, it is thoughts which haven't been birthed. Stillborn sentences from wombs barren due to the smog. Like our mothers', like our grandmothers', generational curses, the double dosing of our poison.

They remind me that tears are water, and water holds toxins. Let it go. That overwork can bring stress, and stress makes you lazy. Let it go. They remind me that if I can in fact breathe I can cackle, let it out and in. That air first must be released, for the next breath to come in, and with hands on my back, whisper "let it all go sis".

They remind me that despite the smog our pretty pink lips can still gossip about sweet kisses from grown ass men. Men who share advice their therapists gave on first dates. They remind me that smog is murky, that we can still sing along to Japanese Denim and keekee about how we aren't ready to forgive Daniel Caesar just yet.

They remind me... I am so much more than smog, so much more than dirt, so much more than soot; and that despite my smog I've never stopped dancing. They dance with me every time, *"cash money records takes over for the 99 and the 2000's."* It is our war cry after a long day's work in the smog.

ASSATA SHAKUR IS
WELCOME HERE

Dear Auntie,

The roses are blooming
in the garden again.

I think of you often, though
maybe not by appellation.

I recognize your influence
in all of my students
with Arabic names.

I wonder if you ever
miss Amerikkka,

or the concrete jungle which
could easily swallow you whole.

I wonder if you've found
a sidewalk near El Malecon

to impress your handprints.

I imagine you've discovered
rueda and guaguancó.

I can envision how regal
you look in all white,
chanting alongside
your hermanas.

"Olugbala gbohun mi,
gbohun mi, gbohun mi."

The Niners played in the
Super Bowl this past February
and you would have been proud

to see all the Kaepernick
jerseys we rocked on that day.

Though it's still sad here
in Oakland sometimes…
Gentrification is the new exile,

and there are more crosses
for black lives every year
at El Dia de Los Muertos
near Fruitvale Station.

But I still feel a sense of pride
when I pass by shops with your face
plastered all over the signs,

and when I see magnificent
roses which dare to reach
past barb wire fences.

Regardless of what
the government says

you are always
welcome here.

COOCHIE CONVERSATIONS

No one is interested in the
black woman's comfort.

No one says excuse me or
moves their cart for her to
pass by in the grocery store.

The manager yells at the black
female cashier while a line full of
customers shake their heads silently.

Co-workers invade her space with
"curious" hands that have never
touched "curly" hair before.

No one gives up their seat for her
on the bus at the end of a shift
when her back is aching and her
eyes are having trouble staying open.

No one praises her for speaking
two languages, code switching to
avoid dangerous situations.

Even brothas pass her on the way home
and yell "bitch" out of the window
when she won't stop to say hello.

Even safe spaces try to
wash her away, mispronounce
her name as colored or brown.

This is why we delight
in getting together.

We talk about coochie
and niggas.

We cackle for hours and joke
about how much more we can
take before we break...

I.

woman will be earth

and you will call her
your gardener.

as her dreams be seeds,
her hands be the shovel.

as the world may give her
nothing but dirt to sow
and nurture,

come spring even the flowers
will lovingly refer to her as
their mother.

but woman will not be an island
nor will she be your warrior,

for woman shall never vanquish
at the palm of any who would
seek to subjugate her,

and to those who cast stone,
and to those who try to destroy
her. i hope you never forget,
that she is also wind and water.

II.

woman will be universe
and you will call her
your totality.

as her heart be moon or sun,
and her intuition be their gravity.

her patterns sustain new life
as her mind shapes an infinity.

for she is matter and the absence of
fertile space full of limitless possibilities.

she does not fear the death of stars
as their soot gathers in her galaxies.

for her blood is their fallen ash
and their existence is her legacy.

but never forget that woman
will also be more than the dust
lingering on top of books, clocks,
and written history.

although her name may be lost
to the worship of words, she will
always be her ancestors' glory.

III.

woman will be god

and you will call her
your creator.

as her breasts be daily bread, and
her womb humanity's shelter.

she will teach her children to flourish
through her care and her nature.

to bring balance to our delicate web,
for that is her purpose and her power.

man shall name her his supple goddess,
and praise the ripe fruits of her labor.

but woman's body will be more than
artists' muse, decorated in tiger
claws and battle scars.

because though our torsos may
be home to both flesh and ichor,

it is our souls that make us truly
ethereal...for they house
entire ecosystems.

*My grandmother's favorite proverb
is one every black woman knows;*

*"you keep your pocket book closed
and you keep it off the floor."*

Dear Jeremy

Salt Lake City, UT

You are the son of a wandering, strawberry blond, deadhead hippie and a dread locked, Rastafarian, rock steady reggae singer. Love, freedom, and truth are in your bones. This shit is in your blood. I was always meant to love you.

A HOME FOR LOVE

When a man loves you
he'll carve himself a home

in your nooks and crannies.

He'll delight in the exploration
of your rivers and valleys,

the natural unspoiled landscape.

He would never call himself
visionary or pioneer, for he knows

that land should not be colonized.

Before I was a voice,
I was a sweet dream
tucked safely inside
my mother's womb.

That's how I know
my pussy tastes
like love. Not guilt,
or shame, or lust.

And if I could re-
trace all of the hands
that have laid their
fingertips into my skin.

I'd plant sunflowers
and fill the crevices
with honey to reclaim
this body for the land.

Call it a diagram
for the bees…

REMATRIATION

MEET ME AT THE RIVER

Make poetry from my skin
by tracing it with the tips
of your fingers.

Read Neruda out loud and
call my brow your wind
and my flesh, your island.

Siempre. Always.

Never forget, my love. That
your arms are my serene refuge,
from the hurricane of weariness,

& I would die content

just for the simple pleasure of
being this present with you
and you only.

Always. Siempre.

BAY TRAIL

Oh hairless boy, who
smells of beard oil,

I will balance my
feet on the anchors
of every shipless
harbor you hitch…

Write you love notes on
ripped receipt papers
and tuck them into the
murky swamp where
you balance your checks.

Brew you coffee, mix
it with sweet water and
place all my bets on you

for this life is bitter
enough already

without love…

FOR DAYS WHEN
I FEAR YOU ARE
JUST A SEASON

I remember,

I am still learning to
write love poems

that are not steeped
in sadness.

Birthed from
my mother's navel.

Traveled through
my father's feet.

I pray to be
more an ocean

than grain of sand
along the beach.

STRING THEORY

There's an infinity
hidden inside
your eyes.

One that stretches
across thousands
of timelines.

An infinity which
can overcome
butterfly effects &
groundhog days.

An infinity filled
with serendipity
where, each time
we meet

as soulmates.

ANOTHER
FOLK SONG

I grew up
in a home
that didn't
believe in love.

But no one ever left,
(until the day that
I did.)

So while I know
I can be loyal,
I'm not sure I've
ever been faithful.

Though I haven't
given up hope
on you
just yet.

"Sometimes in love pain is inevitable but the suffering is discretionary."

Dear Jeremy

Oakland, CA

I knew you loved me when I told you that sometimes I feel like a speck of dust stuck in the great big swirl, and you leaned in to gift me with this, *"Whenever you fear the day, that we all must turn to dust... Remember that you are the dust of stars, and it's to them you must return."*

FLESH

 In this season, I am

learning to be an ocean because
words need time to breathe.

Words need time to be steeped in
experience, baptized in blood, and
unlearned through many tongues.

I have become many things
through undoing;

        be,

            being,

                 been.

But I cannot be a poem
each and every day

for my mind is too often sand,
sometimes trapped in space and

I would no sooner drown in the a b y s s.

Most days, I cannot fathom
becoming an infinity so even
my thoughts become flesh;

and besides…

How can I truly learn to
sing my own praises,

while I am still teaching
myself how to swim?

As far as I know,

and as much
as I can tell

whether I believe in

reincarnation or
heaven & hell.

This is the one time

I will be living this life,
here right now.

So please be fearless and

LIVE WELL.

The Jewelry Blessing Ritual

Need: An intention or mantra & a piece of jewelry.

Steps: Find a mantra that you want to hold on to. For example, one you want to incorporate into your daily practice or an intention for the new moon. Find a piece of jewelry like a bracelet, ring, necklace, etc. Hold the jewelry in your hand(s) and stand in front of a mirror. Repeat the mantra eight times; eight is the number of balance between the physical & spiritual world. Eight also symbolizes infinity, the constant flowing of energy.

Ritual: Put your newly blessed jewelry on and go about your day. Every time you notice the piece either with your eyes or hands, let it be a reminder to pause and observe the lesson or mantra you're holding near. When you find yourself becoming less connected to it, pause to journal, and meditate on the message. What has transformed or manifested since blessing the piece? When the meaning begins to wear, tuck it somewhere safe for future use or even better gift it to someone you love who might be in need of positive energy.

TO WHOM IT
MAY CONCERN,

The greatest learning
in teaching

      is the most intangible

and has everything to do

with feeling.

I hope this message
finds you well…

SURRENDER

I used to think I would
be healed by healing others,

but recently I taped this Zen proverb
over the sink for when I brush my teeth.

> *Knowledge is learning*
> *something every day, but*
> *wisdom is letting something*
> *go*

& I need this daily reminder to reframe
what it means to be empty vs. whole.

When a cup is full you can't
pour in or it overflows...

So, remember this,

you have always been whole
but to truly heal others first

master the process
of *letting go*.

You are not at the whim of the wind. You are the blood of stars. A miracle, a blessing, an offering. A connection to everything that has been and everything coming.

There are no accidents, but maybe serendipitous coincidences.

Never forget, you are abundant, a significant moment in the timeline of the universe.

THE JOURNEY

On the endless
pursuit to thrive,

we claim our crowns
and no one throws
a fucking parade

we collect our flowers
despite the thorns
leaving our palms
bloody and bruised.

We are learning to
recognize patterned
responses

as mental chains
we must break
free from,

in order to become
one with the entire
universe

& this is our
deepest truth.

THE SEED

whenever you find
yourself buried
under the weight
of darkness

remember the seed
waiting patiently
to sprout

yes, there is power
in reaching up
toward the sun

but there is
also, power
in learning

to be still.

FRUIT

been through
so many seasons

fearing you'd never bloom

went around the world and
finally learned the lesson

you were never meant
to be a flower

you have always been

fruit.

I have learned that joy does not always come from happiness, sometimes it comes from healing.

ACKNOWLEDGMENTS

Thanks to everyone on the Nomadic Press team who believed in this book and supported it in coming to fruition. When I started putting the manuscript together, I put Nomadic Press on my vision board as a potential publisher. This book is therefore proof that dreams really do come true! Special thanks to my editor, Michaela Mullin, who poured over the pages with me. And to J. K. Fowler, for creating such a beautiful and dynamic space for writers. One that I am proud to continue being a part of, following publication.

To Black Lawrence Press who supported me in picking up where Nomadic left off. This publishing journey was certainly unlike any other, but I appreciate that you all believed in my work. Having partners in everything from spreading the word, editing, to design really made all the difference and helped keep this writer sane. A shout out to Diane Goettel, who worked tirelessly on all the little details that made this book incredibly special.

Shout out to my MFA cohort at Mills College. X, Chelsea, Thad, and Emilee who each encouraged me in their own unique way as many projects (including this book) were birthed in our year together. Shout out to Dana, Caroline, Em, and Griffin for peer reviewing the final manuscript and giving your precious feedback. To my creative writing professors, Stephanie Young, Keli Dailey, and Truong Tran for your mentorship and guidance.

To Mickalene Thomas whose collage work on the cover embodies all of the nuance I hoped to capture through my words. Thank you for creating work where Black women can see themselves in all our complexities, power, resilience and at times pain that comes with navigating multiple intersecting identities in a place like the United States of America. Your work shows Black women's everydayness and mundanity while highlighting all of our beauty and joy.

To the deep, divine, mystic knowledge of the universe, thank you for allowing there to be flowers, salsa dancing, sisters/cousins/nephews and soul food. Thank you for showing me all of the magic in life that can't be explained by science and logic. The magic which compelled me to jot down notes on napkin scraps and crumpled receipt papers. Thank you to all the cities with unique souls that I called home for days, weeks, and months, while living life on the brink of my own personal revolution.

To my wonderful parents who exemplify strength, stubbornness, and forgiveness.

Most importantly. To my husband. This book should be called, *Dear Jeremy, and All the (Other) Postcards I Never Sent*. I appreciate you for trusting me to tell this story, our story, about one of the most difficult times in our marriage. I am forever grateful that we found our way back to each other and for the relationship we have now, despite the challenges we had to overcome. I am proud that we overcame them together. Thank you for being my eternal muse.

Finally, to all the mags, zines, journals, and other literary communities that gave love to the following poems through their publications:

"Sidewalk Chalk," *Popshot Quarterly*

"The Purge," *Perennial Press*

"The Dandelion Ritual" and "Auntie Gina's House," *Black Freighter Press*

"An Unreliable Narrator," *Allegory Ridge*

"Coochie Conversations," *A Room of Our Own*

"Doing Donuts," *KQED*